Light

Bird Flies South

50395

9 780769 642109

EAN

School Specialty
Publishing

Text Copyright © Alan Durant 2005. Illustration Copyright © Evans
Brothers Ltd. 2005. First published by Evans Brothers Limited, 2A
Portman Mansions, Chiltern Street, London W1U 6NR, United
Kingdom. This edition published under license from Zero to Ten
Limited. All rights reserved. Printed in China. This edition published
in 2005 by Gingham Dog Press, an imprint of School Specialty
Publishing, a member of the School Specialty Family.

Library of Congress-in-Publication Data is on file with the publisher.

Send all inquiries to:
School Specialty Publishing
8720 Orion Place
Columbus, OH 43240-2111

ISBN 0-7696-4210-1

1 2 3 4 5 6 7 8 9 10 EVN 10 09 08 07 06 05

Bird Flies South

By Alan Durant

Illustrated by Kath Lucas

Columbus, Ohio

It was raining.
Bird was wet.

"I am tired of the rain," said Bird.
"I will fly south and find the sun."

He flew until the rain stopped.

"Hooray," said Bird. "I made it south!"

Bump! Thump!
Hail stones hit Bird on the head.

"Oh, no," said Bird.
He flew on to find the sun.

He flew until the hail stopped.

12

"Hooray," said Bird. "I made it south!"

Splat! Splat!
Snowflakes fell on Bird's head.

14

"Oh, no," said Bird.
He flew on to find the sun.

15

He flew until the snow stopped.

16

"Hooray," said Bird.
"I made it south!"

Whoosh! Whoosh!

A great wind blew Bird into the air.

"Oh, no," said Bird.

But the wind stopped.

Bird made it south.
"Hooray!" said Bird.

The sun shone and shone.

Bird grew very hot.

"I am tired of the sun," said Bird.

He flew and he flew.

27

Until he was back home again.

It was raining.

And Bird thought that was just fine.

Words I Know

again	said
find	that
he	very
into	was

Think About It!

1. What happened to Bird first in the story? What happened to him next? What happened to him last?
2. Why did Bird want to fly south?
3. Describe the different kinds of weather in the story.
4. Describe the look on Bird's face on page 21. How do you think he feels at that moment?
5. Bird found out that he was happier back at home. Why?

The Story and You

1. Where would you rather live—where it is very hot or where it is cool and rainy? Why?
2. Have you ever moved away from your home? How did it make you feel?